Level 3

W9-BOL-858

Jumping Josie

A fantasy story

This edition first published in 2006 by
Sea-to-Sea Publications
1980 Lookout Drive
North Mankato
Minnesota 56003

Printed in China

Library of Congress Cataloging-in-Publication Data:

Cassidy, Anne, 1952-
  Jumping Josie / by Anne Cassidy.
    p. cm. — (Reading corner)
  Summary: Josie is a frog who loves to jump, but one day she jumps a little too high and
needs help getting back to her own garden and pond.
  ISBN 1-59771-014-8
  [1. Jumping—Fiction. 2. Frogs—Fiction.] I. Title. II. Series.

PZ7.C26857Ju 2005
[E]—dc22

                                                                    2004063632

9 8 7 6 5 4 3 2

Published by arrangement with the Watts Publishing Group Ltd, London

Series Editor: Jackie Hamley
Series Advisors: Linda Gambrell, Dr. Barrie Wade, Dr. Hilary Minns
Design: Peter Scoulding

For Josie Morey—AC

Jumping Josie

Written by
Anne Cassidy

Illustrated by
Sean Julian

SEA-TO-SEA
Mankato Collingwood London

Anne Cassidy

"I wrote this story after watching frogs leap about in my garden. I hope you enjoy it!"

Sean Julian

"My favourite animals to paint are bears. Frogs are difficult to paint as they jump away!"

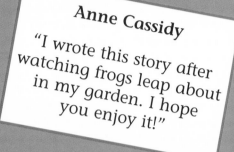

"I can jump higher and higher!"

7

One day, Josie
jumped too high.

She landed in the
next garden!

12

"I don't like this garden,"
said Josie. "There's no
pond and no grass!"

Josie tried to jump back to her own garden.

"The fence is too high!"
she said.

She tried to get through
a hole.

The hole is too small!"
she said.

Josie looked around. She saw just what she needed.

It was a trampoline.
Josie jumped and
jumped and
jumped.

She landed back in the pond in her own garden. Home at last!

23

Notes for parents and teachers

READING CORNER has been structured to provide maximum support for new readers. The stories may be used by adults for sharing with young children. Primarily, however, the stories are designed for newly independent readers, whether they are reading these books in bed at night, or in the reading corner at school or in the library.

Starting to read alone can be a daunting prospect. READING CORNER helps by providing visual support and repeating words and phrases, while making reading enjoyable. These books will develop confidence in the new reader, and encourage a love of reading that will last a lifetime!

If you are reading this book with a child, here are a few tips:

1. Make reading fun! Choose a time to read when you and the child are relaxed and have time to share the story.

2. Encourage children to reread the story, and to retell the story in their own words, using the illustrations to remind them what has happened.

3. Give praise! Remember that small mistakes need not always be corrected.

READING CORNER covers three grades of early reading ability, with three levels at each grade. Each level has a certain number of words per story, indicated by the number of bars on the spine of the book, to allow you to choose the right book for a young reader:

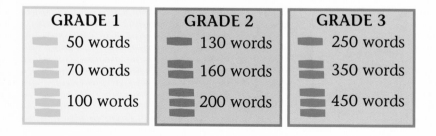

GRADE 1	GRADE 2	GRADE 3
50 words	130 words	250 words
70 words	160 words	350 words
100 words	200 words	450 words